Contents

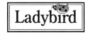

Cover illustration by Stephen Holmes

A catalogue record for this book is available from the British Library

Published by Ladybird Books Ltd
80 Strand London WC2R 0RL
A Penguin Company

4 6 8 10 9 7 5 3

© LADYBIRD BOOKS LTD MM

LADYBIRD and the device of a Ladybird are trademarks of Ladybird Books Ltd

The hairy bear scare

by Clive Gifford
illustrated by Stephen Holmes

introducing the **air** sound,
as in h**air**, b**ear**, wh**ere** and st**are**

3

When Clare came down
the stairs she had
a nasty scare.

For wherever she looked there were bears, bears, bears!

There were bears on the sofa
and bears on the chairs.

Would you care for a pear?

Hairy
Bear
Lair

There were bears
in the cupboard
underneath the stairs.

7

Clare stared at the bears.

The bears stared at Clare.

Clare's bear bared his teeth
and glared.

"How dare you?"
he growled.
"This is MY lair!"

So off they ran those scared
hairy bears.

Dinosaur
at the door

by Naomi Adlington
illustrated by Karl Richardson

introducing the **or** sound, as in
morning, floor, before, claw and pause

One morning, George heard
a knock at the door,

14

and there on the doorstep he
saw a huge dinosaur.

It held out its paw and said,
"Hi, my name is Jaws!

I'm awfully bored – will you play with me outdoors?"

17

Poor George picked himself
slowly off the floor.

He had only seen dinosaurs
in stories before.

George paused, then he looked at the dinosaur's claws.

"You can play on our lawn…

"but *I'm* staying indoors!"

The surfing herd

by Clive Gifford
illustrated by Paula Knight

introducing the **er** sound,
as in surf, herd and swirl

What's that out there?
Oh, my word!

I can see a surfing herd!

They curve and swerve in the swirling surf.

They are so expert that
they never get hurt.

Watch how they turn with a whoosh and a whirl,

riding the waves as they
surge through the swirl.

You won't find this herd grazing on turf.

These cool cows were born to surf.

phonics

Learn to read with Ladybird

phonics is one strand of Ladybird's **Learn to Read** range. It can be used alongside any other reading programme, and is an ideal way to support the reading work that your child is doing, or about to do, in school.

This chart will help you to pick the right book for your child from Ladybird's three main **Learn to Read** series.

Age	Stage	Phonics	Read with Ladybird	Read it yourself
4-5 years	Starter reader	Books 1-3	Books 1-3	Level 1
5-6 years	Developing reader	Books 2-9	Books 4-8	Level 2-3
6-7 years	Improving reader	Books 10-12	Books 9-16	Level 3-4
7-8 years	Confident reader		Books 17-20	Level 4

Ladybird has been a leading publisher of reading programmes for the last fifty years. **phonics** combines this experience with the latest research to provide a rapid route to reading success.

The fresh, quirky stories in Ladybird's twelve phonics storybooks are designed to help your child have fun learning the relationship between letters, or groups of letters, and the sounds they represent.

This is an important step towards independent reading – it will enable your child to tackle new words by 'sounding out' and blending their separate parts.

How phonics works

- The stories and rhymes introduce the most common spellings of over 40 key sounds, known as **phonemes**, in a step-by-step way.

- Rhyme and alliteration (the repetition of an initial sound) help to emphasise new sounds.

- Coloured type is used to highlight letter groups, to reinforce the link between spelling and sound:

and the King sang along.

- Bright, amusing illustrations provide helpful picture clues, and extra appeal.

How to use Book 11

This book introduces your child to the common spellings of the air, or and er sounds. The fun stories will help her* begin reading words including any of the common spelling patterns that represent these sounds.

- Read each story through to your child first. Having a feel for the rhythm, rhyme and meaning of the story will give her confidence when she reads it for herself.

- Have fun talking about the sounds and pictures together – what repeated sound can your child hear in each story?

- Help her break new words into separate sounds (eg. l-aw-n) and blend their sounds together to say the word.

- Point out how words with the same written ending sound the same. If s-urf says 'surf', what does she think t-urf might say?

Some common words, such as 'what', 'said' and even 'the', can't be read by sounding out. Help your child practise recognising words like these so that she can read them on sight, as whole words.

Phonic fun

Playing word games with your child is a fun way to build her phonic skills. Try playing rhyming I-Spy, using words with the air, or or er sound in. Or challenge her to think of as many words with a particular sound in as she can in a minute.